Don't be Afraid to DROP!

published by

National Center
for **Youth Issues**

www.ncyi.org

Duplication and Copyright

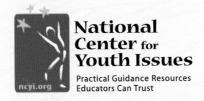

National Center for Youth Issues
Practical Guidance Resources
Educators Can Trust

P.O. Box 22185
Chattanooga, TN 37422-2185
423.899.5714 • 800.477.8277
fax: 423.899.4547
www.ncyi.org

ISBN: 978-1-931636-60-5
© 2008 National Center for Youth Issues, Chattanooga, TN
All rights reserved.

Written by: Julia Cook
Illustrations and Cover Design by Contract: Anita DuFalla
Page Layout by: Phillip W. Rodgers
Published by National Center for Youth Issues
Softcover

Printed by RR Donnelley, Inc.
Reynosa, Mexico
May, 2011

This book is dedicated to Doe June for her genuine insight on life!

About This Book

Writing children's books has given me the opportunity to meet many wonderful people. This book was inspired by a very nice lady that I met on a flight to Dallas, Texas. She told me a story that she would tell to her children whenever they struggled with change. I cannot remember the name of this kind lady, but I think of her often and I would love to meet up with her again someday. We all face difficulties associated with our ever-changing world and we often find ourselves stuck in a rut and afraid to break out of our "comfort zones." As a result, many human gifts are never shared.

 "Thank you my dear friend, for reaching out and sharing your gift with me so that I can now share it with the rest of the world! People understandably might still be nervous and afraid of change, but they may now have the courage it takes to "drop," and expand their horizons."

-Julia Cook

The wind started howling,

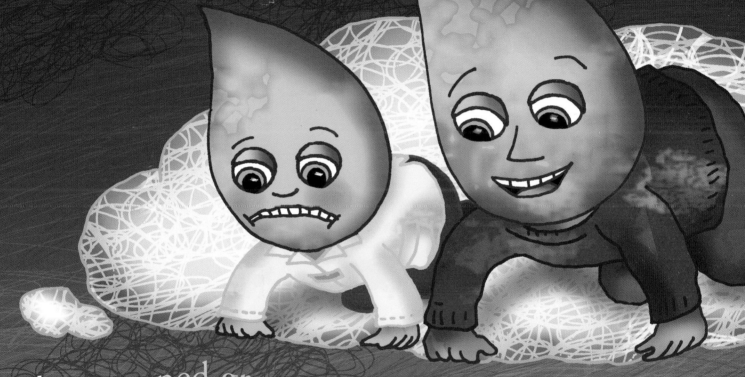

the sky turned grey,

and the rain clouds were full and round.

There stood two raindrops, a father and son,
on their cloud staring down at the ground.

"Our cloud is too heavy. It's your time to drop,"
father raindrop said to his son.

"It's a long way

down

there.

I just *can't* let go!

Are you sure, Dad, that *I'm* the one?"

"I like living here on
our beautiful cloud.
It's all I have ever known.

I'm comfortable here—it's where I belong.

This cloud feels like home."

"You are a raindrop and
all raindrops must fall.

You need to let go
of our cloud.

There's a **BiG** world out there, and you're missing out,

if you choose not
to drop
to the
ground."

"But I have so much fun
on this cloud we live on.

Everyone knows my name.

My life is fine just the way that it is.

Why would I want it to change?

I get to play games
with my raindrop friends.

We skateboard on pillows of air.

We play raindrop baseball

and eat raindrop snacks.

Leaving just

wouldn't be **fair!**"

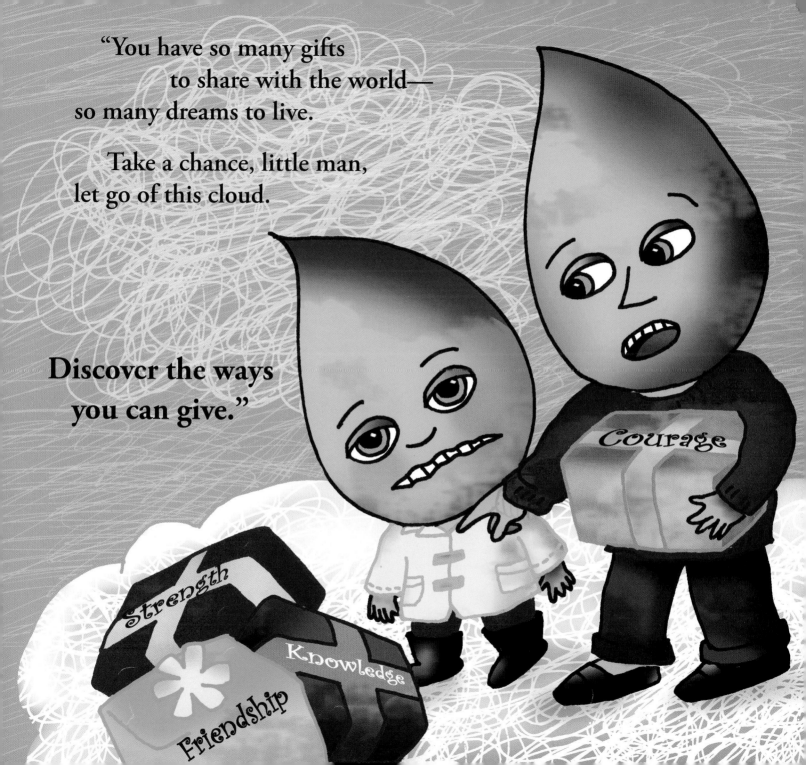

"You have so many gifts
   to share with the world—
so many dreams to live.

   Take a chance, little man,
let go of this cloud.

**Discover the ways
you can give."**

"But I just can't drop! I'm afraid to fall! What if it hurts when I land?

What if I land in a camel's mouth?

What if I land in the sand?

What difference
will I make

if I land in a lake,

where *no one*
will notice me?

You never can tell where you might end up—
but I promise, you'll be just fine.

You will land
where you're needed.

It's OK to let go.

Soon you
will understand.

Our earth needs
your help to make
everything grow,
regardless of
where you land."

"Will you go with me? Can we go together?" boy raindrop asked his Dad.

"You won't have to stay long.

You can leave when we get there,
and then I won't even be sad."

"I cannot go with you. You must drop alone,

but I'll watch you all the way.

You will make me so proud

when you water the earth

on this beautiful, special day."

"I will miss what I have
on this cloud I call home, and

I'm a little afraid to let go.

I'm *nervous* and

scared and

my tummy
has kn_ot_s.

There's so much
out there
I don't know."

"Don't be afraid

to drop

to the

ground.

Be **brave** and **trust**
what I say.

If you don't **take a risk**,
you'll never find out
what great things
might happen today."

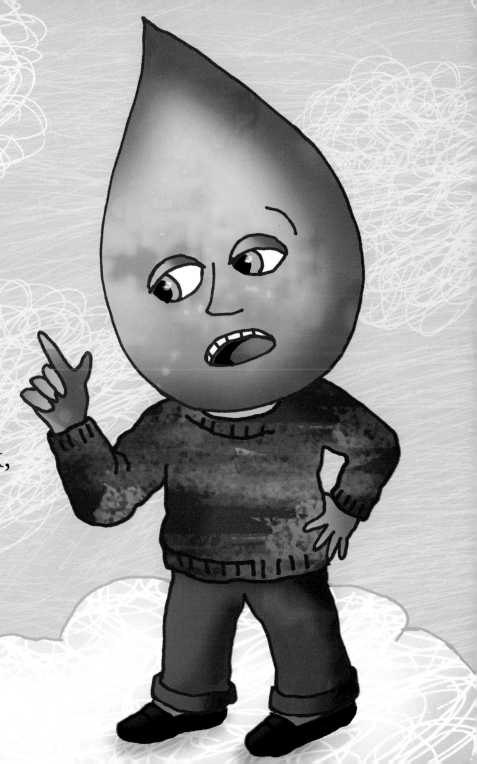

I closed my eyes.
I took a deep breath, and

I let go of my beautiful cloud.

It felt kinda weird

to fall through the air—

but on the inside,

I felt proud.

I'd taken a chance.
I had started to grow.

My purpose in life
would be met.

When I landed, I *Splattered.*

But it
didn't matter.

I'd helped
a dry flower
get wet.

"Thank you so much for sharing your gift."

I heard the dry flower say.

"Now I can grow and
stay healthy, you know—
at least for another day."

Then all of a sudden,

I felt warm inside

as a sunbeam

kissed my cheek.

I started to rise back up to the sky, right past the mountain peak.

When I finally got back
to the cloud I call home,

my dad was there waiting for me.

"I'm so proud of you, Son,
for taking a chance,

and look
who you
turned out
to be!"

Wow!
Wow!
Wow!
Wow!
Wow!

What a difference I had made!
Dropping had helped me to grow.

Change is a good thing
and **giving** feels great!

That's all I needed to know.

Whatever *your* gift is,
whatever *your* purpose,
don't be afraid to let go.

Grab hold of
some courage,
believe in yourself,
and **share** all the
things that you know.

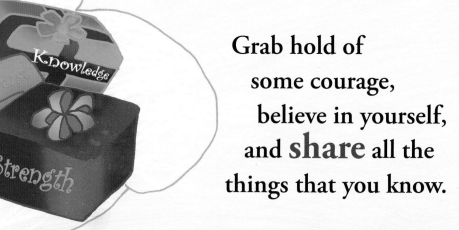